Caillou®
Training Wheels

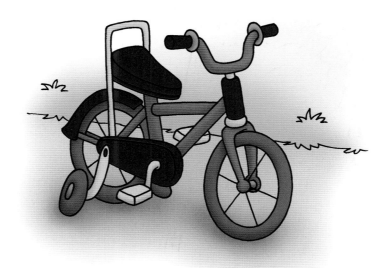

Adaptation of the animated series: Sarah Margaret Johanson
Illustrations: CINAR Animation; adapted by Eric Sévigny

chouette   COOKIE JAR

It was a beautiful day, and everyone was outside.
"Hi, Caillou. Do you want to go for a bike ride?"
Sarah asked, riding up on her bicycle.
"Can I go, Daddy?" Caillou asked.
"Sure. I'll come along, too," Daddy said.

Caillou was trailing behind. Daddy and Sarah were much faster.
Caillou was upset that his training wheels were slowing him down.
"Daddy, can I try riding without my extra wheels like Sarah?" Caillou asked.

"Are you sure you're ready to take your training wheels off?"
"I want to try. Please, Daddy," Caillou said.
"I rode my bike with training wheels for a long time, Caillou.
I only took them off a little while ago," Sarah said.
"I don't need extra wheels," Caillou said.

"All right, let's give it a try. You're going to have to practice and be patient. Switching to two wheels isn't easy," Daddy said.

"Can we go home and take them off right now?" Caillou asked.

"Sure, let's go," Daddy replied.

Back at home, Daddy removed the training wheels from Caillou's bicycle.

"You can do it, Caillou," Sarah cheered.

"Go, Caillou!" Mommy said.

"Yay!" Rosie cried.

"Whoa! Daddy, don't let go!" Caillou said.
Caillou and Daddy went around and around
the driveway.
Daddy was always holding on to the back of
Caillou's bicycle.

"Phew! Let's rest a while," Daddy said.
"I'm not tired, Daddy. Mommy, watch this!" Caillou called
out and took off on his own.
Caillou wobbled and wobbled. He just didn't understand
why he couldn't keep his balance on two wheels.
"I think my bike is getting tired," he said, taking a break.

Later, Mommy asked:
"Caillou, Rosie needs to change her shoes. Can you help her, please?"
"No, I do it, Caillou," Rosie said.
"That's the wrong foot, Rosie. Let me help you," Caillou said.

"Riding without training wheels is hard, isn't it?" Daddy asked.

"Why can't I do it?" Caillou cried.

"Maybe you're just not ready yet," Daddy suggested.

"Like Rosie with her shoes?" Caillou asked.

"Yes. Someday she'll be able to put on her shoes by herself, and you'll be riding that bike all over the neighborhood, you'll see," Daddy assured Caillou.

"Maybe I should keep the extra wheels on for a little while longer," Caillou said. "I think that's a good idea, because you know what? There's a right time for everything," Daddy said.

"Hi, Caillou!" Sarah said. "Want to go for a bike ride?"

"I can't go as fast as you," Caillou replied.

"That's okay, this time I'm not on my bike. I'm just learning to rollerblade, so don't go too fast!"

"Don't worry, Sarah. I won't!" Caillou said.

Text adapted by Sarah Margaret Johanson from the scenario of the CAILLOU animated film series produced by DHX Media Inc.
All rights reserved.
Original story written by Thor Bishopric and Todd Swift
Original episode: "No More Training Wheels" #302
Illustrations taken from the television series and adapted by Eric Sévigny.
Art Direction: Monique Dupras

The PBS KIDS logo is a registered mark of PBS and is used with permission.

We acknowledge the financial support of the Government of Canada through the Canada Book Fund for our publishing activities.

Canadian Heritage   Patrimoine canadien

We acknowledge the support of the Ministry of Culture and Communications of Quebec and SODEC for the publication and promotion of this book.

SODEC
Québec

Bibliothèque et Archives nationales du Québec and Library and Archives Canada cataloguing in publication

Johanson, Sarah Margaret, 1968-
Caillou: training wheels
(Clubhouse)
For children aged 3 and up.

ISBN 978-2-89450-746-9

1. Cycling - Juvenile literature. . I. Sévigny, Éric. II. Title. III. Title: Training wheels. IV. Series: Clubhouse.

GV1043.5.J63 2010   j796.6   C2009-941989-0

Printed in China
10 9 CHO1891 JUL2013